DISCARD

NASHVILLE PUBLIC LIBRARY

MOON LANDING

By Rachel A. Koestler-Grack

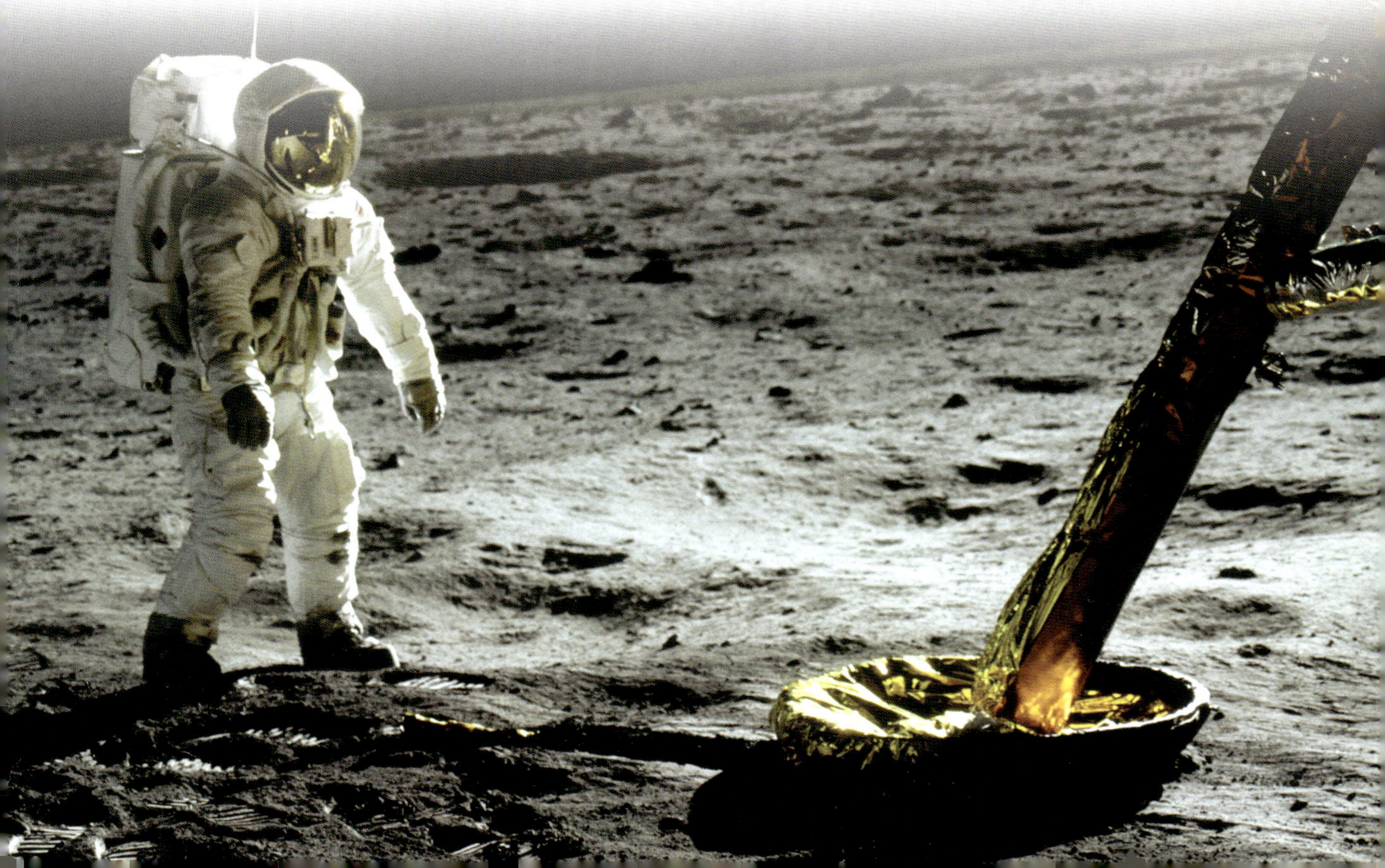

VISIT US AT
WWW.ABDOPUB.COM

Published by ABDO Publishing Company, 4940 Viking Drive, Suite 622, Edina, Minnesota 55435. Copyright © 2005 by Abdo Consulting Group, Inc. International copyrights reserved in all countries. No part of this book may be reproduced in any form without written permission from the publisher. ABDO & Daughters™ is a trademark and logo of ABDO Publishing Company.

Printed in the United States.

Edited by: Melanie A. Howard
Interior Production and Design: Terry Dunham Incorporated
Cover Design: Mighty Media
Photos: NASA, Corbis

Library of Congress Cataloging-in-Publication Data

Koestler-Grack, Rachel A., 1973-
   Moon landing / Rachel A. Koestler-Grack.
     p. cm. -- (American moments)
   Includes index.
   ISBN 1-59197-932-3
   1. Project Apollo (U.S.)--Juvenile literature. 2. Apollo 11 (Spacecraft)--Juvenile literature. 3. Space flight to the moon--History--Juvenile literature. I. Title. II. Series.

TL789.8.U6A5433 2005
629.45'4'0973--dc22

                                                2004061147

Contents

One Giant Leap 4

From Fiction to Reality 8

Moon Vehicles 16

Lunar Landing 22

Other Missions 30

Beyond Apollo 36

Timeline 42

Fast Facts 44

Web Sites 45

Glossary 46

Index 48

ONE GIANT LEAP

On July 16, 1969, American astronauts Neil Armstrong, Edwin "Buzz" Aldrin, and Michael Collins prepared to make history. They lay side by side in their Apollo spacecraft. Soon, *Apollo 11* would take them where no human had ever set foot, the moon.

Half a million people gathered at Cape Kennedy, Florida, to watch liftoff. With four seconds to go, the first stage engines of the Saturn V fired. After the countdown ended, the rocket exploded off the launchpad and burst upward into the sky. One astronaut described the launch this way. He said, "It's like this giant hand grabs the orbiter and throws it into space."

An eagle clutches an olive branch in the emblem of the Apollo 11 mission. The branch represents the peaceful intention of the moon landing.

The trip to the moon took three days. On July 20, Armstrong and Aldrin climbed into the Lunar Module, *Eagle*. They strapped themselves in, still standing, and gazed out of their triangular windows at a strange new world. Aldrin later described the gray and rocky surface of the moon as a "magnificent desolation."

The *Eagle* bounced twice, then landed. The crew opened the module hatch. Armstrong and Aldrin wore bulky space suits that

Launch of Apollo 11

weighed about 280 pounds (127 kg) on Earth. But lunar gravity is only one-sixth of Earth's. The suits would be significantly lighter on the moon.

These special space suits protected the astronauts from the harsh lunar temperatures. At lunar "noon," the temperature rose to a scorching 243 degrees Fahrenheit (117°C). The temperature could drop to 279 degrees below zero (-173°C) at night.

Armstrong made his way down a metal ladder to the lunar surface. On his way down the ladder, Armstrong pulled a cord that started a video camera. From Earth, millions of people watched the historic moment unfold. Armstrong stepped off the ladder, putting his left foot down on the moon. He paused to broadcast, "That's one small step for man, one giant leap for mankind." His print could last for millions of years, untouched by wind or rain.

Aldrin joined Armstrong on the surface. The two men collected samples of moon soil and rock. Armstrong snapped picture after picture of the moon. The men then fixed an American flag on the cratered surface to mark the site. The astronauts later revealed a small plaque attached to the leg of the Lunar Module. It read, "Here men from the planet Earth first set foot upon the moon July 1969 AD. We came in peace for all mankind." The plaque held the signatures of the three *Apollo 11* crew members and U.S. president Richard M. Nixon.

After 2 hours and 21 minutes of moonwalking, Armstrong and Aldrin climbed the ladder into the *Eagle*. They left the moon the following day knowing that their mission had paved the way for other astronauts to return. A world that could once only be reached in the imagination was now open to exploration.

Buzz Aldrin walks on the moon near the American flag.

FROM FICTION TO REALITY

For centuries, people have been fascinated with space travel. In 160 AD, the ancient Greek writer Lucian of Samosata authored what is probably the first story about a journey to the moon, *Vera Historia* or *True History*. It was a satire. His tale was about a sailing vessel that got caught in a violent whirlwind and carried to the moon. The crew met moon creatures and eventually returned to Earth.

A later science fiction story became a surprising prediction. In 1865, Jules Verne published *From the Earth to the Moon*. In this story, three astronauts rode to the moon in a padded, cone-shaped spaceship. The ship was shot out of a 900-foot (274-m) long cannon, *Columbiad*, from Florida. In the tale, the ship made it into space but never landed on the moon. A hundred years later, the first moon-landing flight, *Apollo 11*, launched from Florida in a spacecraft with a cone-shaped nose. Similar to the cannon in Verne's book, *Apollo 11*'s Command Module was called *Columbia*.

Less than 100 years later, technology was catching up with Verne's imagination. On October 4, 1957, the world's first satellite, Sputnik 1, was launched from the Soviet Union. It disappeared in the sky and began orbiting Earth at a speed of 4.9 miles per second (7.9 km/s). Each orbit around Earth took a little over an hour and a half. From Earth, Russian aerospace engineer Sergey Korolyov supervised Sputnik 1's orbit.

IMAGINING THE FUTURE

Many have called Jules Verne the father of modern science fiction. Verne was born on February 8, 1828, in Nantes, France. After studying law, he announced to his parents that he was going to be a writer. During the 1850s, Verne wrote plays, poetry, and some opera. Then in 1863, he wrote the first of 65 voyages extraordinaires, or amazing adventures, for a young readers' magazine. The story was called Five Weeks in a Balloon.

Among his other amazing adventure stories are Voyage to the Center of the Earth, From the Earth to the Moon, *and* Twenty Thousand Leagues Under the Sea. *Verne's most successful novel was* Around the World in Eighty Days, *which he published in 1873. His stories had a strong influence on later authors such as Isaac Asimov. Verne died in March 1905.*

Jules Verne

The satellite put out a constant beeping signal. Sputnik 1 lasted 92 days in space before it fell and burned up in Earth's atmosphere.

The Soviet accomplishment captured the attention of the world, especially the U.S. military. The successful orbit took place during the Cold War between the United States and Soviet Union. These two world powers were engaged in a war of mistrust. The United States accused the Soviet Union of wanting to expand communism throughout the world. In return, the Soviets charged the United States with imperialism and meddling in the affairs of other countries. Battlegrounds were forged in Vietnam and Korea. But the United States and the Soviet Union never directly fought each other.

With the launch of Sputnik 1, Americans worried that the Soviet Union might be able to send bombs to any part of the planet. This fear sparked a frenzy of research, tests, and space launches that became known as the space race.

Launch of Sputnik 1

A month later, the Soviets launched Sputnik 2. This satellite was an even greater accomplishment. At more than 1,000 pounds (450 kg), Sputnik 2 was almost six times larger than the first. More astonishing than its size was Spunik 2's cargo, a small dog named Laika, which means "Barker" in Russian. Laika became the first living thing to orbit Earth. Unfortunately, Laika did not survive the mission. Russians believe she died from overheating in the cabin just hours after the launch.

The United States's first satellite attempt turned into a disaster. On December 6, 1957, the National Aeronautics and Space Administration (NASA) tried to launch the first American satellite aboard a Vanguard rocket. The rocket rose just a few inches, fell, and exploded on the launchpad. Newspapers around the country advertised the failure with headlines such as "KAPUTNIK."

Finally at the beginning of 1958, the U.S. space program regained some pride with the successful launch of Explorer 1. Explorer 1 was followed by many other successful Explorer flights. These missions brought amazing discoveries, including the first photographs of Earth's surface from space.

Yury Gagarin

But the Soviet Union was still a stride ahead of the United States. On April 12, 1961, Russian cosmonaut Yury Gagarin became the first human to orbit Earth. Less than a month later on May 5, the United States answered Gagarin's flight with one of its own. Astronaut Alan Shepard boarded the Mercury spacecraft *Freedom 7* and was blasted 115 miles (185 km) into the sky. Shepard did not make a full orbit like Gagarin had, but the flight was successful.

Later that month, President John F. Kennedy made a surprising speech to Congress. He announced, "I believe that this nation should commit itself to achieving the goal, before this decade is out, of landing a man on the moon and returning him safely to the Earth." Kennedy believed this accomplishment would propel the United States to the front of the space race.

John Glenn became the first American to orbit Earth in February 1962. He made three complete orbits. But scientists still had many questions about the moon. Hundreds of years earlier, Italian astronomer Galileo Galilei observed the surface of the moon through the newly invented telescope. He discovered the moon had a rugged terrain, made up of mountainous ridges and valleys. In the mid-1900s, scientists still didn't know the makeup of the moon.

The U.S. space program would need to conduct in-depth lunar research. NASA started a lunar probe program to find out more about the moon's surface. Scientists developed two kinds of probes, crash landers and soft landers. The crash lander, Ranger, was a "suicide" spacecraft. Its purpose was to take pictures of the moon right up until it crashed. After several failures, Ranger 7 finally hit the moon on target and transmitted more than 4,000 pictures of the moon in July 1964.

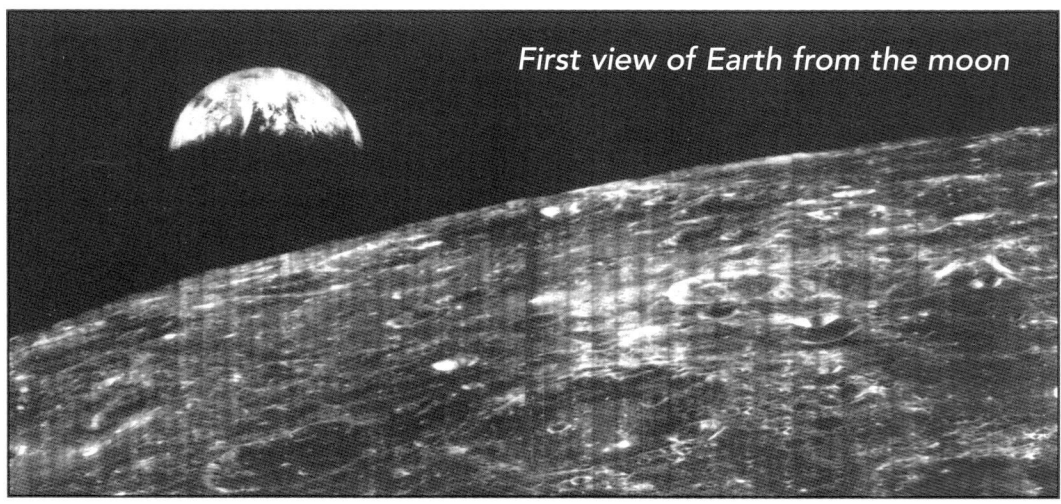
First view of Earth from the moon

John Glenn

    The next step was soft-landing a probe vehicle, Surveyor. Of the seven Surveyor missions, five were successful. Scientists viewed pictures of the moon. They also studied soil samples of a substance called maria taken from the moon with special tools. Maria is the dark, cooled lava that covers 30 percent of the nearside of the moon.

    Once scientists learned it was safe to land on the moon, they needed to select a landing site. Lunar Orbiters circled the moon, taking pictures of possible sites. These spacecrafts helped scientists find the safest landing spots on the moon. With all this information collected, NASA could now begin working on a moon landing.

13

Jay Bodnar wears his space helmet as he watches televised images taken by Ranger 9 in March 1965. Ranger 9 was the final spacecraft in a series of missions designed to photograph the moon. Each Ranger was equipped with six cameras that could take detailed photographs. NASA began lunching the Ranger probes in 1961. The first Ranger missions were unsuccessful. After so many failures, NASA and the public were surprised when Ranger 7 began to record images of the moon. But the project achieved its goals. Rangers 7, 8, and 9 transmitted more than 17,000 images of the moon. Ranger 9 took more than 5,800 photographs before it crashed into a crater.

MOON VEHICLES

The first challenge to getting an astronaut on the moon was building a rocket that had enough thrust to propel a crew and their equipment to the moon. Not even the Soviets had solved this problem. German scientist Wernher von Braun worked out this issue for the United States. He invented the mighty Saturn V rocket to propel the Apollo spacecraft to the moon. At 36 stories tall, Saturn V was the largest rocket ever to fly. The Saturn launch vehicle was specially designed for the trip to the moon.

There were three stages in a Saturn V rocket. The first stage, S-IC, performed the biggest job. It lifted the entire 6-million-ton (5,443,000-t) rocket ship from the launchpad. In only two-and-a-half minutes, S-IC propelled the ship 36 miles (58 km) into the air at a speed of 6,000 miles per hour (9,700 km/h). The power came from five engines at the base of S-IC. Fueled by kerosene and liquid oxygen, these engines together generated 7.5 million pounds (3.4 million kg) of thrust. After S-IC completed its task, it fell into the ocean.

The second stage, S-II, also had five engines, that used liquid oxygen and liquid hydrogen fuel. With 1 million pounds (450,000 kg) of thrust, S-II picked up where S-IC left off. This stage shot Saturn V to about 108 miles (174 km) above ground at about 17,500 miles per hour (28,200 km/h).

Saturn V rocket

Stage three, or S-IVB, had two functions. Using liquid oxygen and liquid hydrogen as fuel, the single engine made two burns. The first burn lasted two minutes and propelled the spacecraft into the proper Earth orbit. Later, a six-minute burn sent the Apollo spacecraft on course to the moon. The spacecraft traveled at about 24,900 miles per hour (40,100 km/h) through space. After the course was set, S-IVB separated from the craft and headed toward the sun.

The Apollo astronauts traveled through space in the Command Module. The Command Module was a cone-shaped capsule specially designed to protect the crew during reentry into Earth's atmosphere. The bottom panel was rounded and covered with an ablative heat shield. Ablative heat shields slowly burn off in the intense heat caused by atmospheric friction during reentry. Flying through Earth's atmosphere at 25,000 miles per hour (40,000 km/h) can create temperatures up to 5,000 degrees Fahrenheit (2,760°C).

Astronauts used two hatches on the Command Module. One hatch, located on the sloped side of the capsule, was for entry at the start of the mission and an exit after splashdown. The second hatch was at the top of the cone. Once in space, Armstrong and Aldrin used this hatch to get to and from the Command Module to the Lunar Module.

A Service Module was attached to the Command Module during the entire mission, except at reentry. The two modules together were known as the Command and Service Module (CSM). The Service Module provided the rocket thrust needed to get Apollo spacecraft into and out of lunar orbit. Later, the 20,500-pound (9,300-kg) thrust engine boosted the astronauts back home. The Service Module housed the tanks of liquid propellant needed to fuel the engine. It also provided breathable oxygen and drinking water for the crew.

Four clusters of four thrusters were attached to the outside of the Service Module. By firing these thrusters, the vehicle could be moved in any direction. This feature was important for plotting a precise path to the moon.

The Lunar Module carried the astronauts to and from the surface of the moon. The Lunar Module consisted of two main parts, the descent stage and the ascent stage. During the launch, the Lunar Module rode beneath the CSM. After leaving Earth's orbit, the pilot docked the Lunar Module to the nose of the Command Module.

When it was time to land on the moon, Armstrong and Aldrin climbed into the Lunar Module, *Eagle*. Like the Service Module, the

Neil Armstrong, Michael Collins, and Buzz Aldrin check the equipment of the Command Module.

Eagle had clusters of maneuvering thrusters. Both the descent module and the ascent module were powered by their own single-rocket engine. At the end of the mission, the descent portion of the Lunar Module served as a launchpad for the ascent module. The ascent module separated from the descent module and climbed back into orbit.

The CSM, the Lunar Module, and the escape tower together stood a mammoth 82 feet (25 m) tall. Attached to Saturn V, the ship was 363 feet (111 m) tall.

LUNAR MODULE CONFIGURATION

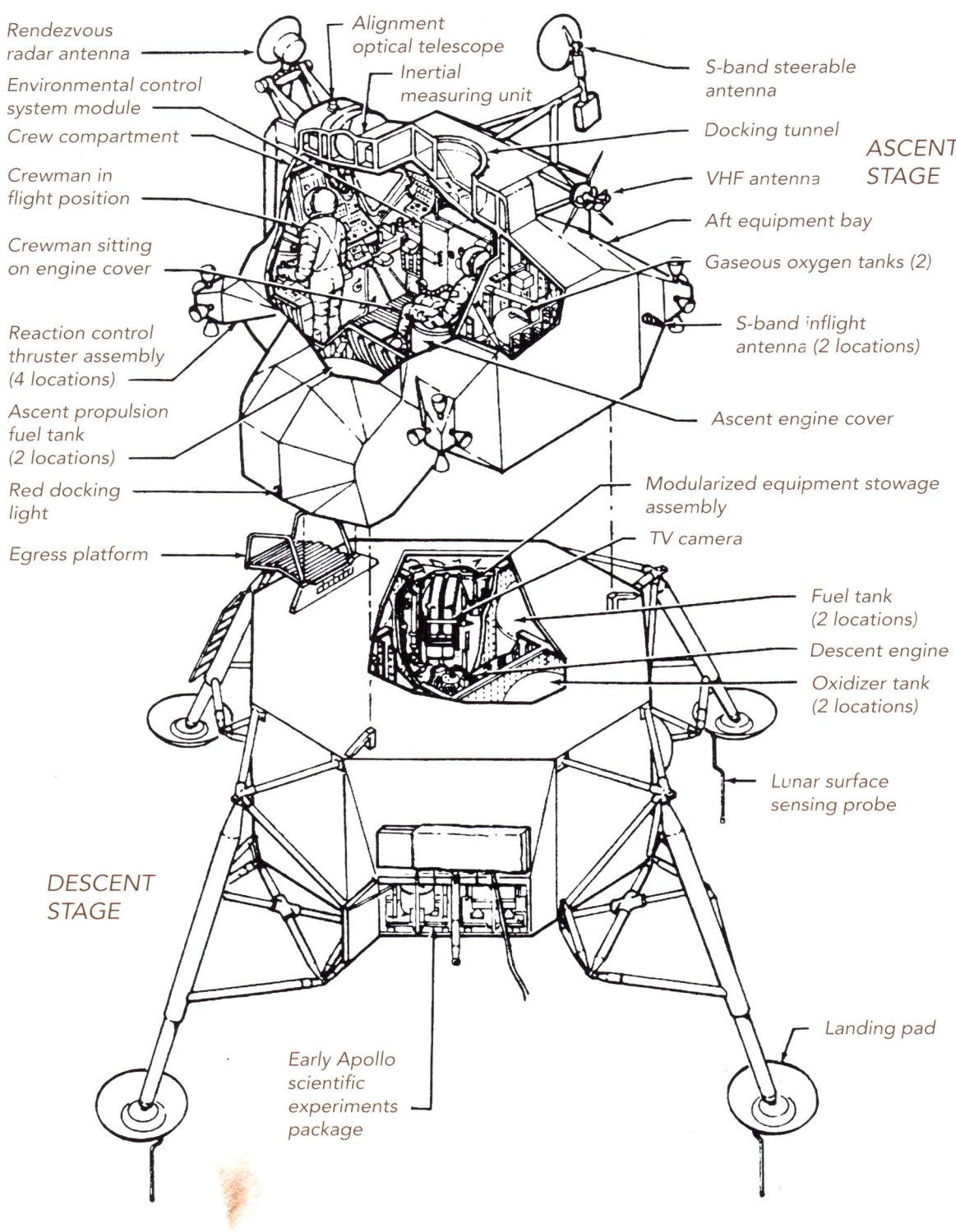

The Command and Service Modules are attached to the Saturn V.

LUNAR LANDING

The United States was making progress, but the space race was not yet won. In fact, the Soviets still had the lead. On March 18, 1965, cosmonaut Aleksey Leonov performed the first space walk. Leonov stepped out of *Voskhod 2* and spent about 10 minutes in space. Americans applauded the amazing feat and quickly returned to their own space work.

NASA launched Project Gemini. During these space missions, astronauts rehearsed many procedures to prepare for the moon landing. In June 1965, Edward H. White II became the first American astronaut to walk in space. He surpassed the Soviet feat with a 23-minute walk.

In February 1966, the Soviets again set the pace. The unmanned Luna 9 became the first probe to land on the moon undamaged. It wasn't until June 1966 that the American Surveyor 1 also made a successful soft-landing. Two months later, Luna 10 became the first unmanned spacecraft to orbit the moon.

The Gemini flights were crucial for landing on the moon. Astronauts expanded on the skills they needed to work in space. They practiced spacewalking, orbital maneuvering, and docking. Docking is the physical connection of two spacecraft in orbit. *Gemini 8* was the first ship ever to rendezvous and dock with an unmanned vehicle in space.

Edward H. White II performs the first American space walk.

The incident almost ended in disaster, however. Neil Armstrong and David Scott successfully linked their spacecraft with an Agena vehicle on March 16, 1966. The two vehicles soon began to roll. At first, the astronauts believed the problem was with the Agena. They separated *Gemini* 8 from the Agena, expecting the problem to clear up. Instead, the rolling worsened. They were spinning at the rate of one revolution per second. Armstrong finally managed to get the ship under control.

Other Gemini missions went more smoothly. After 12 Gemini missions, American astronauts had earned valuable space experience. They had spent nearly 2,000 hours in space. *Gemini* 7 stayed in space for a record-breaking 14 days. This mission proved that a manned vehicle could remain in space for the amount of time it would take to complete a lunar trip.

Only three short years were left in the decade Kennedy promised to send a man to the moon. NASA began the Apollo missions, which would fulfill that challenge. The first Apollo flight was scheduled for February 1967. But tragedy stood in the way. In January, astronauts Virgil "Gus" Grissom, Roger B. Chaffee, and Edward H. White II participated in a plugs-out test of the Apollo Command Module.

A spark set fire to some equipment. The cabin atmosphere was made up of almost pure oxygen, which fed the fire. The hatches on the Command Module were difficult to open. Workers could not get the men out, and the astronauts died. The tragedy delayed the Apollo program. The test was named Apollo 1 in honor of the three astronauts.

Virgil "Gus" Grissom, Edward H. White II, and Roger B. Chaffee

Three months later, the Soviets had a tragedy of their own. Cosmonaut Vladimir Komarov was killed testing a new spacecraft, the *Soyuz-1*. Komarov's superb piloting managed to get him safely back into Earth's atmosphere. But his parachute became entangled with the spinning ship. He crashed into the ground.

Despite the Apollo 1 disaster, the United States continued on its space quest. In November 1967, the Saturn V had a test launch. The sound at liftoff was deafening. For miles around, the ground rumbled and shook like an earthquake. Despite the noise, the Saturn V performed well. It launched the first manned Apollo craft, *Apollo 7*, into an Earth orbit mission in October 1968.

In December, the United States launched *Apollo 8*, the first flight to the moon. Astronauts Frank Borman, James A. Lovell, and William A. Anders became the first humans to make this historic trip. However, this journey did not include a lunar landing. *Apollo 8* made ten orbits around the moon, then returned to Earth. Lovell described Earth as viewed from the moon as "a grand oasis in the big vastness of space."

NASA sent up two more test missions. Crews practiced rendezvous and docking in lunar orbit. They rehearsed every procedure. Nothing could be left to chance during the moon landing.

Then on July 16, 1969, the United States launched *Apollo 11*. This time, the crew would be landing on the moon. The target site was in the Sea of Tranquillity. Armstrong, Aldrin, and Collins traveled to the moon without problems. On July 20, the Lunar Module separated from the CSM. Astronaut Michael Collins kept the CSM in orbit while the Lunar Module descended to the surface.

As Armstrong and Aldrin watched the moon come closer and closer they came to an alarming realization. The crew had overshot their planned destination. Now they were headed straight for a boulder field. Armstrong took over the controls from the module's computer. Amazingly, the Lunar Module touched down on the moon unharmed. Armstrong radioed back to Earth, "Houston, Tranquillity Base here. The *Eagle* has landed."

Only 22 hours later, Armstrong and Aldrin began their ascent back to the CSM. The module lifted into space without incident. After the astronauts reached orbit, the CSM maneuvered to the Lunar Module and safely docked. Michael Collins thought, "We really are going to carry this off!" After eight days in space, the Command Module splashed down in the Pacific Ocean on July 24.

Americans hailed their new heroes. Armstrong, Aldrin, and Collins were honored in parades in major cities across the country. The world also celebrated with the United States. The three astronauts visited 23 countries during a 45-day tour. The Soviets, however, were less than thrilled. They continued to develop their space program, but gave up trying to send a man to the moon in 1974.

Neil Armstrong, Michael Collins, and Buzz Aldrin

Neil Armstrong gathers equipment from the Lunar Module, *Eagle*. Behind Armstrong is the American flag and the Solar Wind Collector. Edwin "Buzz" Aldrin had set up the collector earlier. It was a foil sheet that was pointed in the direction of the sun. Before they left, Armstrong and Aldrin rolled the collector back up. Scientists would later examine the particles on the foil.

Other Apollo 11 mission experiments included the passive seismograph experiment (PSE) and the laser ranging retroreflector (LRRR). The PSE was set up to monitor moonquakes and meteor impacts on the moon. The LRRR used laser beams and reflection to measure the exact distance from the moon to Earth. It also took other measurements, such as the radius of the moon.

OTHER MISSIONS

The *Apollo 11* moon landing was a historic achievement unmatched by any other. But space research was far from over. NASA planned to continue sending spaceships to the moon.

On November 14, 1969, *Apollo 12* was launched into a stormy sky. Shortly after liftoff, a lightning bolt knocked out the ship's electrical systems. In a panic, the mission was almost abandoned. The crew reset the circuits and power returned. With all systems back to normal, the mission was a go.

During this journey, astronauts hoped to bring back parts of a Surveyor spacecraft. Scientists wanted to study the equipment after long-term exposure to the lunar environment. NASA planned to set the Lunar Module down in the Ocean of Storms. The lunar landing was remarkably accurate. Astronaut Peter Conrad spotted "Old Surveyor" not far off on the surface.

The crew also brought along a nuclear-powered Apollo Lunar Surface Experiments Package (ALSEP). This

Peter Conrad sets up the ALSEP.

Photograph of a moon rock taken during the Apollo 12 mission

piece of equipment was the first of five long-term scientific stations on the moon. Each ALSEP contained instruments for measuring sound waves in the soil, moonquakes, and heat levels in the soil.

The astronauts soon returned to Earth. They had collected samples equaling 75 pounds (34 kg) of rock and soil. Scientists found that the rocks collected from the Sea of Tranquillity were 3.7 billion years old. The rocks collected by *Apollo 12* were 3.2 billion years old. This discovery meant the Ocean of Storms lava spills took place 500 million years after the spills at the Sea of Tranquillity. The rocks were chemically different as well. In other words, the moon had not been a solid and unchanging body.

 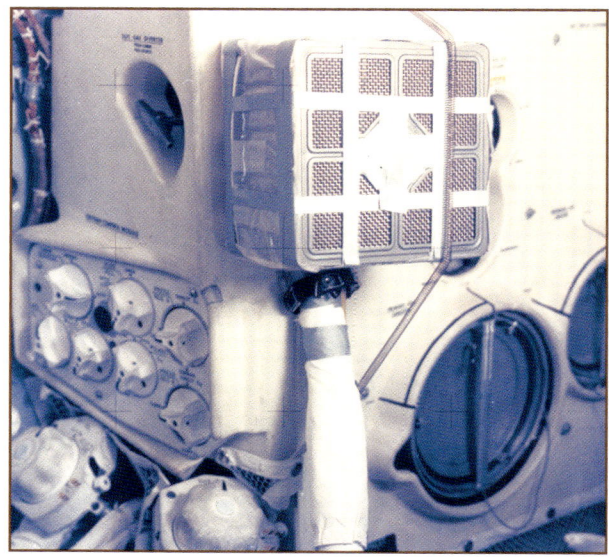

The Apollo 13 *crew members assemble a filter. The completed filter appears on the right.*

With this new information, *Apollo 13* was set to land away from the other spots. Its target was a hilly area called the Fra Mauro Formation. Scientists hoped to obtain new information about the moon's makeup.

Apollo 13 lifted off on April 11, 1970. For the first two and a half days, the flight proceeded flawlessly. Suddenly, crew members heard an explosion. Astronauts John L. Swigert Jr., Fred W. Haise Jr., and James A. Lovell shut down the Command Module's remaining systems. They wanted to save the remaining power for reentry to Earth's atmosphere.

The three men quickly realized their only chance of survival was in the Lunar Module, *Aquarius*. They would have to spend the next 90 hours cramped in a spacecraft designed to hold two men for 45 hours. Furthermore, they had to conserve their limited battery power by shutting down all systems but those absolutely necessary. The cabin temperature quickly fell to just above freezing with these heat-generating devices off.

The biggest problem facing the astronauts was a lack of oxygen. *Aquarius* did not have enough filters to produce enough breathable air for the return trip. The square Command Module tanks did not fit in the round holes of *Aquarius*. Using a space suit hose, cardboard maps, plastic bags, and tape, the crew members managed to make the square filters fit.

Amazingly, *Apollo 13* made it safely back to Earth on April 17, 1970. Even though the ship never made it to the moon, the courage and skill of Swigert, Lovell, and Haise made them heroes of survival. Less than a year later, *Apollo 14* made a successful trip to Fra Mauro.

The Apollo 13 Command Module is recovered after splashdown.

On July 26, 1971, *Apollo 15* rocketed toward the moon. This time the target was the mountainous region of Hadley-Apennine. The Apennines is one of the largest mountain ranges on the moon, with Mount Hadley reaching nearly 15,000 feet (4,570 m). During this trip, astronauts used a new type of vehicle called a lunar rover. This four-wheeled space car resembled a dune buggy, which earned it the name Moon Buggy. It had a top speed of 8 mph (13 km/h).

As astronauts rolled along the hilly terrain of the moon, video cameras captured lunar mountains, boulder fields, and canyons. The crew collected valuable rocks, including the Genesis Rock. This crystalline rock was about 4.5 billion years old, nearly as old as the moon itself.

Two more moon missions followed. On April 21, 1972, *Apollo 16* touched down at the moon's highland region of Descartes. The final lunar voyage of the twentieth century began on December 7, 1972, with *Apollo 17*'s liftoff. This crew searched for evidence of active volcanoes. Unfortunately, the astronauts did not find any. But they did find an orange substance that had been exposed by a meteor impact.

Before the crew made its final ascent, astronaut Eugene Cernan uncovered a plaque on the spacecraft leg. He broadcast the words to Earth. "Here man completed his first exploration of the moon, December 1972 AD. May the spirit of peace in which we came be reflected in the lives of all mankind," the plaque read. *Apollo 17* splashed down in the Pacific Ocean at 2:25 PM on December 19. The Apollo era had ended.

Astronaut Eugene Cernan rides on the lunar rover.

BEYOND APOLLO

The Apollo program opened up an amazing world of space exploration. Sixty scientific experiments probed the moon's surface. Thirty more studies took place in the Command Module during lunar orbits. Apollo astronauts brought back a total of 841 pounds (381 kg) of lunar rock samples. This lunar data helped scientists conclude that the moon has a rigid crust 20 to 40 miles (32 to 64 km) deep, four times thicker than Earth's crust. They believe the crust is made up of lightweight matter that floated to the surface when the moon was still a molten, volcanic mass during the Age of Formation.

For hundreds of years, people thought the moon remained unchanged since its formation. The Apollo program revealed a different story. Apollos 14 and 16 found rocks that proved there had been volcanic eruptions many centuries ago. The moon's history is imprinted on its surface like a scar on skin. Unlike Earth, wind, rain, and inhabitants do not reshape it. Scientists can study its evolution as though it is a picture taken billions of years ago.

The Apollo program planned for 20 missions. Flights 18, 19, and 20 held fantastic possibilities as technology became more advanced. Landing sites included the far side of the moon, where the soil was of a different type. There is little maria on the far side of the moon. At

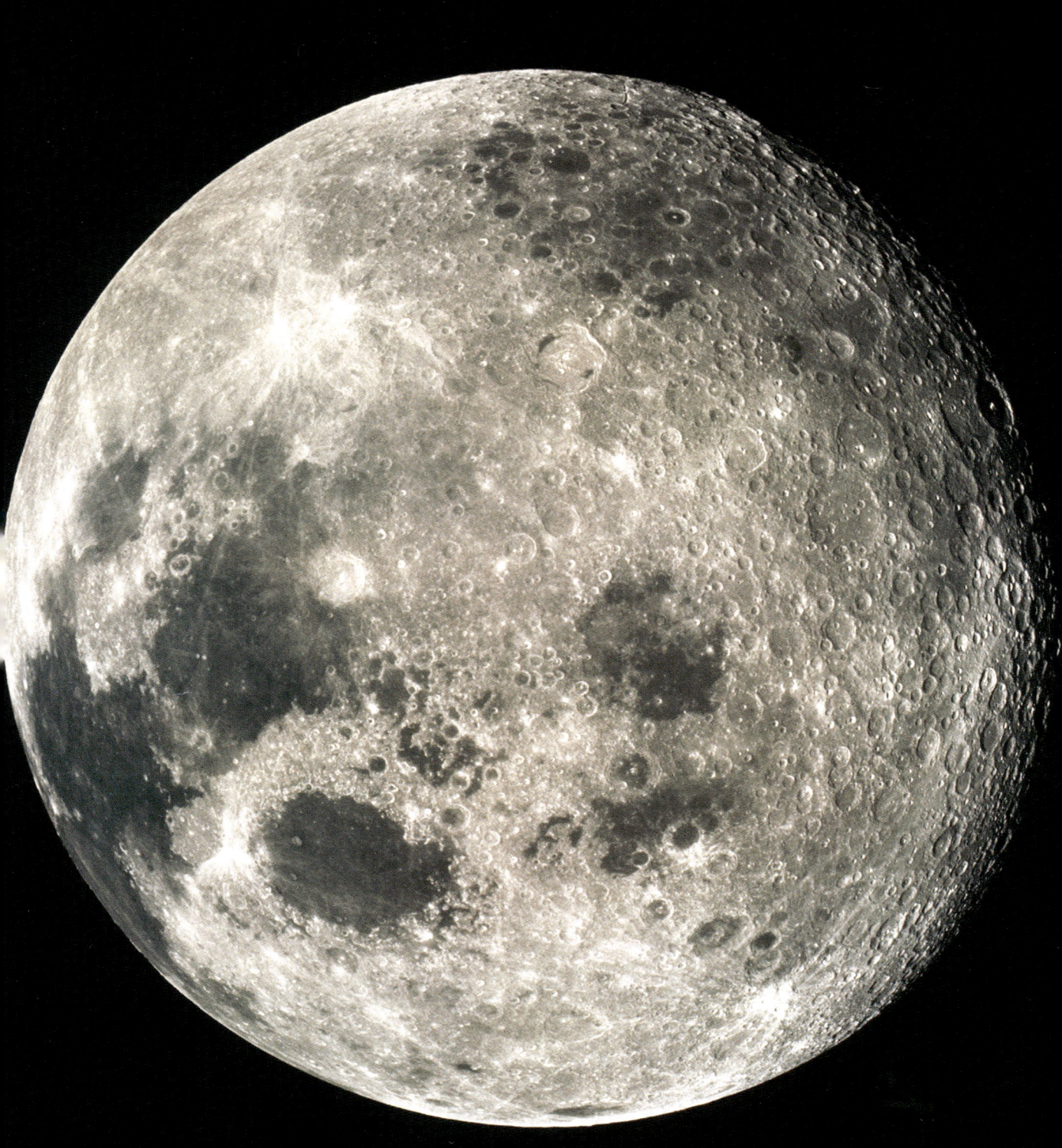

The moon

first, this idea was dismissed. On the other side of the moon, astronauts would lose contact with Earth. Later, NASA decided it could launch communication satellites into lunar orbit, which would retain contact.

NASA had visions of grander surface transportation. Scientists wanted a vehicle that could travel farther than the Moon Buggy. They also wanted to develop better life-support packs for the astronauts so that they could stay on the lunar surface longer. Some scientists wanted to design a two-seated lunar flyer, or a "Mooncopter." Although the flyer was a dangerous concept, astronauts couldn't wait to see it created.

If astronauts could stay on the moon longer, many more experiments could be conducted on missions. Engineers wanted to design an unmanned Lunar Module that could land ahead of the crew. This "lunar truck" would carry a huge load of supplies. Another idea was a lunar laboratory vehicle. This vehicle would have a pressurized cockpit in which the astronauts could live and breathe. They could travel long distances without having to return to the spacecraft every day.

These ideas could extend a mission from days to weeks. There were many extraordinary sites on the moon to explore. Astronauts wanted to visit the polar regions, which might contain frozen water. They could visit areas too dangerous to land a spacecraft, such as the Straight Wall. This enormous cliff runs in nearly a straight line for dozens of miles.

However, political decisions and budget cuts forced NASA to turn its attention to a new project, the Skylab space station. The public had lost interest in the moon. But the Soviets were building a space station to orbit Earth, which opened up a new competition.

Skylab

    Although the Soviet Salyut 1 became Earth's first space station on April 19, 1971, NASA was proud of Skylab. Because the Saturn V gave the United States more launching power, Skylab was much larger than Salyut 1. It had more than 12,700 cubit feet (360 cu m) of living space. Astronaut sleeping quarters took up the two lower decks. The quarters included a bathroom, shower, exercise station, and science station. Two great solar wings extended from either side of Skylab to provide solar power.

    Skylab would use stage three of a Saturn V to house it as it launched into orbit. This station would remain in Earth's orbit, and crews could visit it and conduct countless experiments. Three labs were built, two to launch, and one for training.

39

In 1973, the first unmanned Skylab blasted into orbit. As always, the Saturn V performed perfectly. But Skylab suffered some damage. The atmospheric pressure ripped away part of the station's outer covering. One solar wing tore off completely, and the other wing failed to open. With little solar power, the station was in immediate danger.

The first Skylab crew planned to launch the following day. But their launch was delayed as NASA engineers worked around the clock to find a way to fix the crippled station. Ten days later, the crew headed for Skylab. Astronaut Peter Conrad from the Apollo 12 mission led the first crew. Their first task was to get the station repaired and working properly. When they arrived, they found the station temperature at a sweltering 100 degrees Fahrenheit (37.8°C). They set up a huge foil umbrella to shield the tears in the station's outer shell. The temperature quickly dropped.

Wearing his bulky Apollo space suit, Conrad began one of the most crucial space walks in history. He managed to get a solar wing to extend. Skylab was designed to have full power with only one working wing. Conrad and his crew had saved the day. They enjoyed a month's stay on the first American space station.

NASA soon developed other ambitions. Future goals included a permanent base on the moon and a manned mission to Mars. Whether or not these goals will ever become a reality is unknown. They would be very challenging. But, as President Kennedy fearlessly said, "We choose to go to the moon in this decade—and do the other things—not because they are easy but because they are hard."

Buzz Aldrin's boot print on the lunar surface

TIMELINE

1957 — On October 4, the Soviet Union launches Earth's first satellite, Sputnik 1.

The Soviet Union puts a dog named Laika into space. Laika becomes the first living thing to orbit Earth.

On December 6, the United States's first satellite blows up on the launchpad.

1961 — On April 12, Yury Gagarin becomes the first human to orbit Earth.

On May 5, Alan Shepard becomes the first American in space.

In a speech before Congress, President John F. Kennedy challenges the United States to land an astronaut on the moon.

1962 — In February, John Glenn becomes the first American to orbit Earth.

1965 — On March 18, Aleksey Leonov performs the first space walk.

In June, Edward H. White II becomes the first American to spacewalk.

1967 — In January, the Apollo 1 disaster takes the lives of Virgil "Gus" Grissom, Roger B. Chaffee, and Edward H. White II.

1968	In December, the first manned Apollo spacecraft is launched.
1969	On July 16, *Apollo 11* blasts off for the moon.
	On July 20, Neil Armstrong becomes the first human to walk on the moon.
	On July 24, the *Apollo 11* Command Module splashes down in the Pacific Ocean.
1970	In April, *Apollo 13* is damaged and must return to Earth without landing on the moon.
1972	In December, *Apollo 17* becomes the last Apollo mission to the moon.
1973	NASA launches Skylab.
1974	The Soviet Union decides not to send a cosmonaut to the moon.

American Moments

FAST FACTS

The Apollo program is named after a Greek god. Besides being the sun god, Apollo was also seen as the god of travelers and emigrants. The name was suggested by one of the National Aeronautics and Space Administration (NASA)'s early members, Abe Silverstein.

It takes astronauts 45 minutes to put on their space suits. They then must wait another hour inside the suit before exiting the spacecraft to walk on the moon. In total, 12 people have walked on the moon, two from each successful Apollo landing.

The *Apollo 11* crew had two different meals to choose from during their mission. Meal A consisted of peaches, bacon squares, coffee, sugar cookie cubes, and a pineapple-grapefruit drink. Meal B had cream of chicken soup, beef stew, grape punch, date fruitcake, and orange drink.

After the *Apollo 11* Command Module was recovered, the three astronauts were quarantined for three weeks, just in case they were contaminated with dangerous moon germs. This later proved to be unnecessary.

During the Apollo 14 mission, astronaut Alan Shepard hit a golf ball on the moon. He is the only person to have ever done this. He fitted an 8-iron head to the handle of a lunar sample collection device and hit three golf balls. The balls are still there.

WEB SITES
WWW.ABDOPUB.COM

Would you like to learn more about the moon landing? Please visit **www.abdopub.com** to find up-to-date Web site links about the moon landing and other American moments. These links are routinely monitored and updated to provide the most current information available.

Buzz Aldrin in the Apollo 11 Lunar Module

GLOSSARY

ablative: removed by evaporating, cutting, or friction.

aerospace engineer: an engineer who makes airplanes or spaceships.

capsule: a pressurized compartment that can detach from a larger craft.

communism: a social and economic system in which everything is owned by the government and given to the people as needed.

cosmonaut: an astronaut from the Soviet Union or Russia.

desolation: devastation or ruin.

imperialism: one country imposing its power on another country to gain control of that country's resources or politics.

lunar: having to do with the moon.

module: part of a space vehicle that can detach and be piloted separately.

oasis: a place in the desert with water, trees, and plants.

pressurize: to maintain a normal atmospheric pressure.

probe: a device used for testing substances and transmitting information from space.

rendezvous: a maneuver in which spacecraft approach each other in space.

satire: writing that makes fun of qualities of human life.

terrain: the physical features of an area of land. Mountains, rivers, and canyons can all be part of a terrain.

INDEX

A
Agena Vehicle 24
Aldrin, Edwin "Buzz" 4, 6, 18, 26, 27
Anders, William A. 26
Apollo 1 24, 25
Apollo 7 25
Apollo 8 26
Apollo 11 4, 6, 8, 26, 30
Apollo 12 (craft) 30, 31
Apollo 12 (mission) 40
Apollo 13 32, 33
Apollo 14 33, 36
Apollo 15 34
Apollo 16 34, 36
Apollo 17 34
Apollo Lunar Surface Experiments Package (ALSEP) 30, 31
Apollo program 4, 16–18, 24–27, 30, 32–34, 36, 40
Aquarius 32, 33
Armstrong, Neil 4, 6, 18, 24, 26, 27

B
Borman, Frank 26
Braun, Wernher von 16

C
Cape Kennedy 4
Cernan, Eugene 34
Chaffee, Roger B. 24
Cold War 9
Collins, Michael 4, 26, 27
Columbia 8
Conrad, Peter 30, 40

E
Eagle 4, 6, 18, 19, 26
Explorer 1 10

F
Freedom 7 11

G
Gagarin, Yury 11
Gemini 7 24
Gemini 8 22, 24
Glenn, John 12
Grissom, Virgil "Gus" 24

H
Haise, Fred W., Jr. 32, 33

K
Kennedy, John F. 11, 12, 24, 40
Komarov, Vladimir 25
Korea 9
Korolyov, Sergey 8

L
Leonov, Aleksey 22
Lovell, James A. 26, 32, 33
Luna 9 22
Luna 10 22
Lunar Orbiters 13
lunar rover 34

M
Mercury project 11

N
National Aeronautics and Space Administration (NASA) 10, 12, 13, 22, 24, 26, 30, 38–40
Nixon, Richard M. 6

P
Project Gemini 22, 24

R
Ranger 7 12
Ranger probes 12

S
Salyut 1 39
Saturn V 4, 16, 17, 19, 25, 39, 40
Scott, David 24
Shepard, Alan 11
Skylab 38–40
Soviet Union 8–11, 16, 22, 25, 27, 38, 39
Soyuz-1 25
Sputnik 1 8–10
Sputnik 2 10
Surveyor 1 22
Surveyor probes 13, 30
Swigert, John L., Jr. 32, 33

V
Verne, Jules 8
Vietnam 9
Voskhod 2 22

W
White, Edward H., II 22, 24

48